Produced by The Creative Spark
San Clemente, California

Illustrated by Yakovetic Productions

Printed in the United States of America.

ISBN 1-56326-155-3

Flounder,
My Hero

"Isn't it beautiful?" exclaimed the Little Mermaid. The treasure she held was made out of silver and gold and ivory and glass, and sparkled and shined in the sunlight.

"It sure is!" agreed Flounder the fish. "What is it?"

"It's a compass," Ariel explained. "Humans use them to find their way home when they're lost. See this arrow? It always points north no matter which way you hold it."

"We'll just see about that," said Scuttle the seagull, taking the compass from Ariel.

He spun around and around in circles as fast as he could, trying to trick the compass. But no matter how fast he spun, the arrow in the compass still pointed north. "Well, what do you know!" he said. "It really works!"

"Be careful, Scuttle!" Sebastian cried, as he watched Scuttle teeter along the edge of the lagoon. But he was too late. The dizzy bird tripped and fell, and the compass plunged deep into the water.

"Don't worry, I'll get it!" Flounder said, diving into the lagoon.
He searched and searched, but the compass was nowhere to be found.

Those two mischievous eels, Flotsam and Jetsam, had already found Ariel's compass and hidden it inside a cave.

"I wouldn't go in there if I were you," the eels warned Flounder when they saw him swimming toward the cave. "A monster lives in there."

"A m-m-monster?" Flounder said, his voice cracking.

"Yes," hissed Flotsam. "A big, *hungry* monster!"

"And it's just about his dinner time, too," added Jetsam.

"I don't believe you," Flounder said, mustering all his courage. "There's no such thing as monsters."

"See for yourself," replied the eels.

Flounder peeked inside the cave. There was something in there, all right, because a huge eye was staring right back at him!

The little fish was so scared that he turned around and swam back to the lagoon just as fast as he could.

"What's the matter, Flounder?" Ariel asked when he returned. "You look like you've seen a ghost!"

"Worse!" Flounder blurted out. "A m-m-monster!"

"A monster!" chuckled Sebastian. "Why, there's no such thing!"

"But I saw him!" Flounder cried. "He was huge, and he had this one giant, ugly eye and big sharp teeth."

No one would believe Flounder's story about the monster. Not even Sandy.

That night, Flounder's dreams were filled with monsters. He swam and he swam, but he couldn't get away from them!

The next day his sister Sandy sneaked up behind him and shouted, "Boo!" Poor Flounder was so scared that he leapt nearly three feet out of the water. "What a little scaredy-fish!" she teased him. "You're afraid of your own shadow!" Sandy laughed and laughed until her sides hurt.

"Cut it out!" Flounder pouted. "That's not funny!"

"Guess what?" Sandy called out as she swam away. "There's no monster and I'm going to prove it!"

"Where are you going?" Flounder asked nervously.

"To the cave!" Sandy said. "Maybe you're afraid, but *I'm* not!"

Flounder swam to Ariel's grotto as fast as he could. "Ariel!" he cried. "Sandy's going to the monster's cave! You have to stop her!"

The Little Mermaid laughed. "How many times do we have to tell you, Flounder?" she said. "There are no such things as monsters."

"Well, if you won't help me, maybe Sebastian will," Flounder said.

Now that Sandy had reached the cave, she wasn't feeling so sure of herself. It was dark and spooky, and the water surrounding it was icy cold. "Hello?" she said softly, peering inside. "Is anybody in there?"

Sandy swam into the mouth of the cave. It was so dark that she knocked some rocks down across the entrance. Suddenly, there it was—Flounder's monster! And it was looking straight at her!

Sandy tried to turn and swim away, but she got stuck between the rocks in the mouth of the cave. No matter how hard she pushed and wriggled, she couldn't get out.

Meanwhile, Flounder had found Sebastian and was asking for his help. Just then, they both heard his sister's cries. "Help!" she shouted. "Help! I'm trapped!"

"Oh, no! The monster's got Sandy!" Flounder said. "I have to save her!"

"Wait for me!" cried Sebastian, clutching Flounder's tail as the little fish sped away.

"Don't worry! I'll get you out of there!" Flounder called.

"Hurry, please!" Sandy cried. Flounder quickly began pulling away the rocks that trapped his sister.

Soon Sandy was able to wriggle free. "Oh, thank you, Flounder!" she said. "You saved me from the monster!"

"Monster, eh?" Sebastian said as he poked his claw inside the cave and pulled out the compass. "Here's your monster!"

"Ariel's compass!" Flounder exclaimed. "But I was sure I saw a monster!"

"I saw it, too!" Sandy said.

"What you saw was the reflection of your own eye in Ariel's compass," explained Sebastian. "So you see, there never was a *real* monster after all."

"All this time I was afraid of a little piece of metal and glass," Flounder said glumly. His fins drooped and his tail dragged along the ocean floor as they reached Ariel's grotto.

"You should be proud of yourself, Flounder," the Little Mermaid said. "When you thought your sister was in trouble you went to her rescue, and that was a very brave thing to do."

"Hey, that's right! When it really counted, I *was* brave!" Flounder said, as he puffed out his chest.

"I'm sorry I teased you," Sandy said, giving him a big kiss. "You're not a scaredy-fish. You're my hero!